The Nutcracker

Jan Burchett and Sara Vogler
Illustrated by Richard Johnson

Clara was fed up. She wanted to go to a theme park but Uncle Fergus had come to stay.

Uncle Fergus had brought presents. He gave Mum a tin of elephant sweets. He gave Dad a yellow tie. He gave Grandad a kit to make aliens.

Then Uncle Fergus gave Clara a box. In the box was a strange little man with a funny arm.

"What is it?" asked Clara.

"It's a nutcracker," said Uncle Fergus. "You put a nut under its arm and crack the shell, like this. You'll love it!"

Uncle Fergus winked at Clara.

Then he whispered, "It's a magic nutcracker. It will help you sleep and give you wonderful dreams."

But Clara didn't want a nutcracker. It didn't look magic – and she hated nuts. So she hid it.

That night, Clara couldn't sleep, so she went
downstairs to get the nutcracker. Perhaps it would
help her to sleep after all.

But the nutcracker wasn't there. Clara looked
everywhere, but she couldn't find it.

All at once there was a flash of light and Clara began to shrink! Everything around her looked huge.

Then she saw one of the aliens that Grandad had made. It was enormous! It reached out and tried to grab her. Clara had nowhere to run.

She was trapped!

Suddenly, there was a yell from above.
"Nutcracker Man to the rescue!"
Clara looked up. It was her nutcracker. The
alien gave a roar and jumped on the nutcracker.

But Nutcracker Man took the alien under his arm and cracked him. The alien broke into little pieces.

"That was cracking good fun!" said Nutcracker Man.

"How did you do that?" gasped Clara.

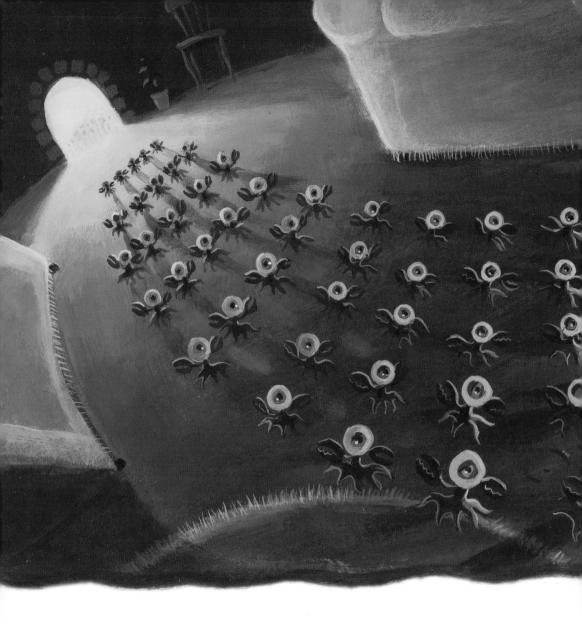

"No time to tell you now!" cried Nutcracker Man.
An army of aliens was marching towards them.

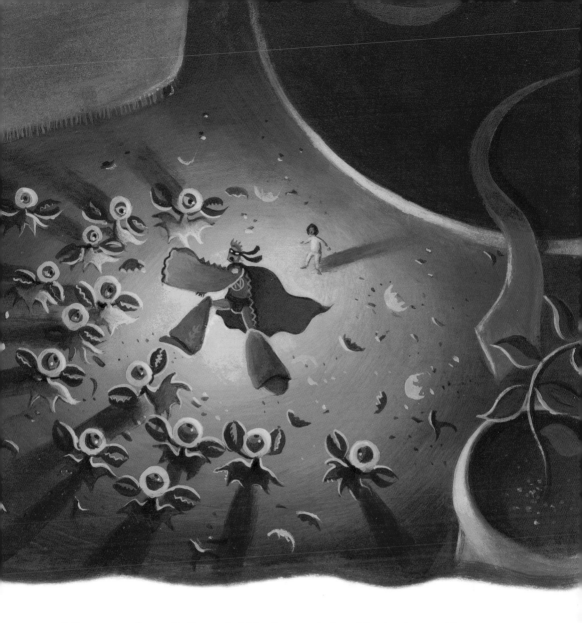

Nutcracker Man biffed and boffed the aliens.
He cracked them with his nutcracker arm.
But the aliens kept coming. Nutcracker Man
was in trouble!

Clara quickly climbed up Dad's new tie and on to the table. She opened the tin of elephant sweets and dropped them down on top of the aliens. Soon all the aliens were trapped in the sticky goo.

"I've won!" yelled Nutcracker Man.

"We've won!" said Clara.

Clara slid back down the tie and looked at the horrible mess on the floor.

"No time to clear up," said Nutcracker Man. "It's time for some cracking good fun."

He grabbed Clara by the hand and they shot up the chimney.

Nutcracker Man took Clara to a wonderful theme park.

They climbed on to the biggest rollercoaster in the world. The rollercoaster zoomed up and down and looped the loop, over and over again.

Then something went wrong. The rollercoaster whizzed down and down into the dark, and it didn't stop!

"We're going to crash!" yelled Clara.

There was a flash of light and …

Clara was lying on the floor holding the little
nutcracker.

"What's going on?" cried Dad.

"Have you been here all night?" said Mum.

Uncle Fergus winked at Clara.

"Did you have a good dream?" he asked.